CONTENTS

TIGER WARRIOR
BATTLE FOR THE JADE RABBIT

For Lois

ORCHARD BOOKS

First published in Great Britain in 2023 by
Hodder & Stoughton

1 3 5 7 9 10 8 6 4 2

Text © Orchard Books Ltd 2023
Cover and inside illustrations by Alan Brown
represented by Advocate Art
© Orchard Books Ltd 2023

The moral rights of the author and illustrator have been asserted.

All characters and events in this publication, other than those clearly
in the public domain, are fictitious and any resemblance to real
persons, living or dead, is purely coincidental.

A CIP catalogue record for this book is available from the British Library.

ISBN 978 1 40837 091 9

Printed in Great Britain

MIX
Paper from
responsible sources
FSC
www.fsc.org
FSC® C104740

The paper and board used in this book are made from
wood from responsible sources

Orchard Books
An imprint of Hachette Children's Group
Part of Hodder & Stoughton Limited
Carmelite House, 50 Victoria Embankment, London EC4Y 0DZ

An Hachette UK Company
www.hachette.co.uk
www.hachettechildrens.co.uk

PROLOGUE

It was the eve of the Moon Festival and a huge full moon slowly began to appear from behind large clouds. All seemed well in the Jade Kingdom as preparations for the festival got underway. But on the side of a craggy mountain overlooking the palace, something lurked in the shadows. The silence was broken by the spine-chilling sound of heavy breathing. Something was sniffing the air like a dog hungry for its bone.

As the clouds moved across the evening sky, the moon cast its glow on the creature. It was the hideous floating head of the Taotie monster! There were no eyes on its green scaly face and its gaping jaw was packed full of razor-sharp teeth. Slimy drool dripped from its terrifying mouth, pooling on the floor. Taotie's nostrils flared; it could smell something familiar in the air. And it knew it was no longer alone.

Out of the shadows, a sinister voice boomed, "It's almost time, Taotie!" The

Dragon King moved out of the shadows and faced the monstrous floating head. "I will give you your body back. But in exchange, you shall do my bidding. Without your body, you cannot see, and without your body, you cannot eat. Are you willing to become my servant?"

The floating monster's head nodded. It was very hungry. What it wanted to do more than anything was to FEAST!

"So be it! Be whole once again!" The Dragon King clapped his hands in a thunderous roar. In a flash, Taotie's body returned to its head. The body had four legs with sharp claws, and huge eyes bulged at the top of the shoulders. Taotie could see again! It blinked and looked around the mountainside. It could run! Taotie ran in a circle and roared with glee! It had been many years since it had been able to move properly. Being a floating head was no fun at all. The monster had spent most of its time hiding in the darkness on the mountainside, away from the world. The creature began sniffing the air in search of food for its empty belly.

"Enough playing around!" the Dragon King commanded. "Now you must repay me for making you whole."

The monster stood to attention. Its new master was right. It was time to wreak havoc, and Taotie was hungry for anything and everything.

"Look down there," the Dragon King ordered, pointing at the palace in the distance.

Taotie's bulbous eyes blinked at the sight of a thousand lanterns twinkling in the dark.

"When this night is over, no one will be able to defeat me," the Dragon King continued. "Not even that pesky Tiger Warrior. For you and I shall have everlasting life, and I will create an army of immortals!" The Dragon King's eyes sparked and he gave an evil cackle.

The monster licked its long fangs with its red tongue. The Dragon King stroked its head and whispered an order in its ear. Then he pointed to the palace. Taotie nodded and bounded down the mountain towards the glistening lights of the Moon Festival.

CHAPTER ONE

As Jack entered the Chinese supermarket, he was hit with the familiar smells of ginger, spring onions and freshly baked egg custard tarts. He picked up a shopping basket.

"No, that's too small!" said his grandad, Yeye. "We need a trolley to carry all the things we have to get for the Moon Festival." Yeye looked at the shopping list that Jack's mum had given him. "We have to get paper lanterns and lots of mooncakes. And we need to get those special mooncakes with ice cream inside for your cousin Marcus because they're the only ones he'll eat. Thankfully, there are so many varieties these days. I like the traditional ones with egg yolk in the middle. What's your favourite?"

"I'll eat any of them," Jack said, grinning. "Red bean paste, lotus paste, matcha ice cream and the egg ones. I love them all!"

'You remind me of a beast I once fought," said Yeye. "It would eat anything in sight. But I'll tell you about that another time." Yeye winked at Jack. Not long ago, Jack had learned that he was the Tiger Warrior, a defender of the Jade Kingdom – just as Yeye had been, and just like Jack's father, Ju-Long, had been.

Jack loved hearing his grandad talk about his time as the Tiger Warrior. – and he had already had some amazing adventures of his own in the Jade Kingdom with Princess Li and the zodiac animals. He wished he knew more about his dad's time as the Tiger Warrior, but Yeye didn't talk much about those years.

As Jack put some ice cream mooncakes

in the trolley, he wondered if Marcus would want to play *Jungle Quest* when he came round. Marcus was his cousin on his mum's side. He was way taller than Jack and one year older, and he was always boasting that he was better at gaming than Jack. Jack hadn't made it past the basketball level in *Jungle Quest* and Marcus loved to tease him about it. Jack wished he could tell Marcus that, as the Tiger Warrior, he could harness the power of the zodiac animals and had fought beasts that Marcus could only dream of. But Yeye told him that he had to keep it a secret, to keep everyone in the family safe.

"Yeye, tell me again, why is there a rabbit on these lanterns?" Jack asked, picking up a red paper lantern with a gold rabbit on the side. Red tassels hung from the bottom.

"One of the Moon Festival legends is of the Jade Rabbit who lives on the moon with the moon goddess, Chang'e," Yeye replied.

"Is the rabbit her pet?" Jack asked.

"Oh no." Yeye laughed. "The Jade Rabbit is much more important than that. It's the only creature in the Jade Kingdom that knows how to make the elixir of immortality."

"What's the elixir of immortality?" Jack asked.

"It's a magical potion that allows people to live forever."

Jack stood open-mouthed for a moment. If only his dad could have had some of the magical elixir, then the evil Dragon King wouldn't have been able to kill him.

"But enough about that," Yeye said.

"We need to get this shopping back before the guests arrive!"

Once they'd got everything on the list, they headed outside to the car. It was getting dark and the pearly moon was huge in the sky. Jack squinted, trying his hardest to see the goddess Chang'e and the Jade Rabbit. He didn't think he'd like living up there. He couldn't imagine

living anywhere without his games console or his favourite snacks.

When Jack and Yeye arrived home, Jack's mum, Laura, was serving drinks to her sister, Auntie Sarah, and her husband, Uncle David. Marcus was already playing on the games console.

"You've grown loads, Jack," said Auntie Sarah, messing up his hair.

"I'm still much bigger than him though," said Marcus as Jack sat down beside him on the sofa. "Hey, have you got to the final level on *Jungle Quest* yet?" But before Jack could answer, his cousin started speaking again. "I have, twice at least. I can help give you some tips on the best way to do it if you like? I defeated the King of the Jungle so easily the last time I did it."

Jack squirmed. He hadn't passed level two yet. When he was in the form of the orangutan avatar, he always he always got stuck on the basketball level and lost a life.

"Right, I'm going to set up the table outside. Could you please put up the lanterns?" Jack's mum said to Yeye.

Yeye nodded and followed her into the garden.

"There's only one controller here," said Marcus, "You'll need to get another one so I can beat you!"

Jack rolled his eyes, wondering why Marcus always had to be so big-headed. "OK, hang on. I'll go and get the other one from my room. Then I'll show you who's going to be beaten!" he added as he hurried upstairs.

As soon as Jack entered his bedroom, he knew something was up. He had the strongest feeling he was needed in the Jade Kingdom. Jack fetched the Jade Coin out from under his pillow. He had to keep it hidden, because how could be explain to anyone apart from Yeye that the Jade Coin opened a portal into the Jade Kingdom, and that he was its sworn protector, the Tiger Warrior?

As he held the coin up, he saw that it was glowing. He knew it. He was being summoned to the Jade Kingdom!

CHAPTER TWO

Jack tossed the coin into the air and
commanded, "JADE KINGDOM!" In an
instant, the familiar circular portal began
to open, growing bigger and bigger.
Jack peered through and saw a long
procession of people, many carrying
lanterns. A few people near the front of
the procession held a huge fire dragon

made of straw and golden sticks. Jack was buzzing – this looked more fun than gaming with his big-headed cousin. *If only Mum could experience this*, Jack thought. But even his dad had kept the Jade Kingdom a secret from her.

Now Jack was the protector of the Jade Kingdom, he felt so lucky to have a second home. The best thing was, he could have fun in the Jade Kingdom *and* make it back in time for the Moon Festival celebrations. Time passed differently in the Jade Kingdom, so he could squeeze in a real adventure before playing *Jungle Quest* with Marcus. And it would be great to get away from his cousin's boring boasting for a while.

Jack hopped through the portal and instantly smelled the delicious street food on offer. The Jade Kingdom was alive with chatter, laughter and people hanging lanterns everywhere. Children ran through the streets holding paper rabbits on sticks with ribbons trailing behind. Just then, the coin in Jack's hand began to glow. He knew what that meant! One by one, the zodiac animals appeared. Jack was pleased to see them. Goat smiled at Jack and greeted the Tiger Warrior with her mind.

Welcome back! she said telepathically.

Snake slithered up and brushed her

head against Jack's arm. "Sssssssoooo
good to see you again, Jack. We've
misssssed you."

"It's great to be back," Jack replied.
"The kingdom looks amazing. It beats my
back garden anytime!"

Monkey leapt out in front of Jack

and hugged him. But before Jack even had time to say hello, Monkey started swinging from one lamp-post to the next with his super-long arms.

"Monkey, where do you get your energy from?" Jack laughed.

"Ooh, mooncakes everywhere!"

Monkey said, extending an arm and sneaking a mooncake from one of the stalls. Quick as a flash, he stuffed it into his mouth and swallowed it in one huge gulp. Monkey was often teased by the other animals for not having a flashy superpower, but he was definitely the most athletic and he could make his arms very long. Monkey liked to joke that this meant he was great at stealing things. Yeye always said that stealing was bad, but if it was from a bad guy then it was OK.

"Hey, you didn't get me one," said Pig, looking very disappointed.

"Sorry," Monkey replied. "My arms

have a mind of their own sometimes."
His smile faded. "Oh dear, I'm not very
useful, am I?"

"Of course you are!" Jack exclaimed.
"None of us can swing all over the place
like you, and those extendable arms will
come in handy one day. Don't you worry."
Jack wished he had Monkey's energy and
athletic ability when he did P.E. at school.
It would be so much easier to dunk a
basketball with Monkey's special arms.

"Wow, I love the dragon the villagers
have made!" Dragon exclaimed. She
curled her long scaly body in front of Jack
to get a better view of the huge dragon
dancing at the front of the procession.

Jack was about to ask what they should go and see next when he spotted something glowing in the night sky. It was coming closer and closer. The zodiac animals formed a protective circle around Jack in case there was trouble.

"Ah, don't worry everyone!" Dog cried. "It's Princess Li flying in!"

Jack smiled. When his friend Princess Li transformed into her phoenix form, the Fenghuang, she could soar through the sky. She was also an excellent fighter. Jack had learned a lot about combat from the Princess. She landed next to Jack and the animals, then transformed before their eyes into her human form. She was wearing a red top and gold trousers that glimmered in the lamplight.

"Jack, you made it!" Li said, giving him a hug. "I summoned you because I thought you would like to join our Moon Festival celebrations. It's such a wonderful evening, especially later when the lanterns all 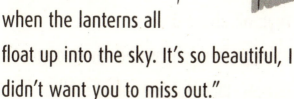 float up into the sky. It's so beautiful, I didn't want you to miss out."

"I can't wait to see how you celebrate here," Jack said. "Yeye and my mum are

31

organising a little celebration right now in our back garden, but it's nothing like this!"

Princess Li gave Jack a lantern from one of the stands and took one for herself. "Let's join the lantern procession."

Jack took the lantern and followed Li. The animals followed too. The air was filled with the sweet smell of incense and fried food. Jack made a mental note to tell Yeye all about it.

As the procession carried on through the streets, Jack noticed many stalls full of delicious mooncakes in every colour. There was even more variety than in the

Chinese supermarket back home. Each mooncake had a different pattern on top and the smell was amazing. Pig ventured near one of the stalls. Jack knew he was hungry. But then he noticed a tall figure in a long black cape standing at the stall. A large hood hid what appeared to be a huge head. A hand darted out of the cape and grabbed some mooncakes. *What a greedy so and so*, thought Jack. Mooncakes were so rich and heavy that even one was too filling for Jack to eat all by himself. But this person was helping himself to loads.

"That guy over there loves food as much as I do," said Pig, pointing one of his front trotters at the caped figure.

Jack laughed. "Yes, you're right. I hope they leave enough for everyone else."

Monkey began hopping on the spot and squealing.

"What's wrong, Monkey?" Jack asked, but Monkey kept squealing and waving his long arms at the stall. Jack wondered if he was jealous that the man was eating a lot.

Princess Li gave Jack a look as if to say, *Please make Monkey be quiet.*

Jack held out the coin and said, "MONKEY RETURN" and Monkey disappeared back into the Jade Coin.

Just then, the procession turned the

corner and they were in front of the Jade Palace. The full moon was high in the sky and a silence came over the crowd. Li ushered Jack and the remaining Zodiac animals to a private area near the palace steps.

"This is going to be special!" Li said. They all stood, staring in anticipation as the Jade Emperor came out of the palace. Suddenly, a beam of white light shone down from the moon. It was brighter than Jack had ever seen and people covered their eyes as it got closer and closer.

"Is that who I think it is?" Jack gasped. Princess Li nodded.

There, floating above the steps of
the Jade Palace, was the moon goddess,
dressed in celestial green, and next
to her was a rabbit as white as snow.
Just like the rest of the crowd, Jack was

speechless. Even Goat and Rat were silent. They all bowed down as the goddess placed her feet on the ground.

Princess Li leaned over and whispered into Jack's ear, "It's really her – it's Chang'e and her beloved Jade Rabbit. Every year during the Moon Festival, the people of the Jade Kingdom come to honour her."

"I can't believe it!" Jack whispered back. "I'm actually here with the moon goddess! Wait until I tell Yeye." He thought back to earlier, when he had been trying to make out their shapes in the moon but all he could see were strange squiggles. Now the goddess was standing next to the Jade Emperor right in front of him, and the Jade Rabbit was there too!

CHAPTER THREE

Jack wondered if Yeye had met Chang'e
in real life too. He was sure Marcus would
never believe him if he told him.

"Welcome back, Jack. Let me introduce
you to Chang'e and the Jade Rabbit," said
the Jade Emperor. As the zodiac animals
moved closer to get a better look, the
Jade Rabbit hopped into Chang'e's arms.

"Very pleased to meet you!" the moon

goddess said. "I've heard a lot about the latest Tiger Warrior. You seem to be doing a fabulous job."

Jack felt his cheeks blush hot. "Thanks a lot, but it's a team effort," he said.

"Everyone gather around as I tell the story of how I met the Jade Rabbit," the Emperor called. Jack and Li went to sit next to him and Chang'e on the stage.

"One day, a long, long time ago, I decided it was the right time to prepare an elixir of life for immortality," the Emperor began. "However, humans appeared to be too selfish and untrustworthy for such a job and I thought a gentle animal might be better.

So I came down to Earth pretending to be a beggar and went into the forest, searching for the right animal. I cried out for help, telling the creatures that I was hungry and frail. Soon, three animals came to my side – a monkey, a fox and a rabbit. Each went in search of food for me. The monkey bought fruits from the trees and the fox came back with a fish from the stream. But the rabbit couldn't find any food from the woodland floor. When he returned, empty-handed, the rabbit felt bad that he'd been unable to help. Then the rabbit had a thought – what if he offered himself up for dinner? But I couldn't eat the poor little rabbit, so I immediately turned back into the Jade Emperor. I knew I had found the most loyal and selfless creature. I carried him up to the moon and there we began the mission of making the elixir of immortality, safe from any human who might wish to steal such an important potion."

As the Jade Emperor finished telling his tale, the audience burst into applause and the Jade Rabbit leapt out of Chang'e's arms and started hopping around the stage in glee. Jack and Princess Li laughed as the rabbit forward-rolled and sprang up. But then the crowd's cheers turned to murmurs of concern. Jack looked over to see someone shoving people out of the way as they ran towards the stage. It was the hooded figure with the huge head who had taken lots of mooncakes earlier. But before Jack could utter a word, the figure flung off the black cloak and leapt on to the stage next to the Jade Emperor and the now trembling white rabbit.

Jack gasped in shock. It wasn't a person at all! It was a monster with green skin, standing on its hind legs. Its mouth was like a gaping cave and its roar was deafening. Jack glanced at its sharp, pointed teeth. They put Tiger's teeth to shame and were covered with

bits of chewed up mooncake. The monster's eyes weren't on its head but bulged instead at the top of its front legs. Jack had never seen a creature like it in all of his life.

"It's Taotie!" cried Princess Li. "My father banished it to the mountains many years ago. It's one of the four evils, known for its greed. My father took its body away to stop it from eating everything – and everyone."

"Does it eat ... humans?" Jack asked, very worried that this might be his last Moon Festival celebration. Princess Li nodded. Jack gulped.

"It looks ravenous!" said Rat.

"How did it get its body back?" Li muttered.

"Don't worry, Jack, we're here!" said Dragon. The rest of the Zodiac animals gathered round and Monkey reappeared from the coin. He wrapped his very long arms around Jack's shoulders and gave him a squeeze.

"How is this possible? How did you

get your body back?" the Jade Emperor spluttered to Taotie. He moved in front of Chang'e, trying to protect her from the foul beast.

"The Dragon King kindly put me back together and now I'm so hungry!" Taotie snarled, coming closer and closer to the Jade Emperor.

Jack's stomach churned at the mention of the Dragon King, the evil fiend who had killed his father. The monster took another step towards the Emperor, its drool dripping on the floor. Li ran to stand next to her father. Jack did the same.

"It cannot be!" said the Jade Emperor. Taotie turned away from the Emperor

and set its bulbous eyes on the Jade
Rabbit. Chang'e ran forward to protect
her companion. But it was too late. Taotie
quickly grabbed the shivering white
rabbit in its claws, then bounded from
the stage and raced back through the
stunned and scared crowd.

"No!" Chang'e cried.

Jack, Li and the Jade Emperor watched in horror as Taotie disappeared into the night, taking the Jade Rabbit with it.

CHAPTER FOUR

Chang'e stumbled back and sat down with a defeated look in her eyes. "My beloved friend. He's gone ..." she whispered.

The Jade Emperor went over to comfort her. Jack wished he could have done something. But it all happened too quickly and he hadn't realised the monster was after the Jade Rabbit.

"Don't worry, we will return the Jade Rabbit to you. Won't we?" the Jade Emperor said, turning to look at Jack. "We've got the Tiger Warrior here ready to fight!"

Li patted Jack on the arm. Jack nodded, but he was unsure if he could defeat the man-eating beast. Taotie was clearly very strong and very fast.

"Er … yes … I'll do my best," he stammered. "And so will the zodiac animals." The animals all nodded in agreement.

Please, you must get him back!" Chang'e cried.

The Jade Emperor helped her stand up.

"I'll take her inside. You two get the Jade Rabbit back," he said to Jack and Li. They nodded, and the Jade Emperor and moon goddess hurried into the palace.

"I'll fly over the crowd and see if I can find him. It's not going to be easy, but with the light of the moon we might just spot him," Princess Li said.

"Good idea. I'll ride Horse and see if I can find him on the ground," Jack said. He put the other zodiac animals back into the coin and jumped on Horse. "Let's go!"

The crowd parted to make a path for Jack and Horse to speed through and they pointed in the direction they had seen the evil creature go.

"That way ..."

"Over there ..."

"The beast went that way ..." they cried.

"By the mooncake stand," Fenghuang squawked overhead.

Jack saw them! The Jade Rabbit was beating his little furry legs against the monster's side, but it was making no difference. The Taotie was greedily shovelling mooncake upon mooncake into its huge mouth. It was like a bottomless pit. People screamed and ran indoors to hide from the beast.

Jack breathed a sigh of relief. If Taotie

was eating the mooncakes, then it wasn't going to eat the Jade Rabbit – at least not yet. And it gave him some time to come up with a plan. Jack got off Horse. Which animal should he call upon next? He looked at Taotie's gaping mouth and had an idea. He took the coin from his pocket and summoned Tiger.

"Tiger transform!" he said quietly, not wanting Taotie to hear. As soon as he'd uttered the command, his hands and feet became paws and his skin became covered with stripy fur. The spirit of Tiger had entered his body and he was filled with the wildcat's power. Careful not to make a sound, Jack padded over to the mooncake stall. Li hovered overhead in her phoenix form. Jack waited for Taotie to grab some more mooncakes, then he raised his tail and took aim. As the monster's huge mouth opened, Jack flicked his tail towards it. A ball of fire went flying from his tail and through the air. Jack held his breath and waited.

Would it hit the target?

"Yes!" he exclaimed as the fireball went flying through the rows of spiky teeth. If only he could use Tiger's power when he was shooting hoops on *Jungle Quest* against Marcus!

"Good shot, Jack," Li cried, landing beside him and changing back into her human form.

Taotie screamed in agony as flames lit up his mouth. Letting go of the Jade Rabbit, the monster grabbed a jug of juice from the stall and poured it down its throat. A cloud of steam hissed from Taotie's mouth as the flames went out.

Jack turned back into his human form

and ran over to the Jade Rabbit. But before he could save it, a black cloud covered the moon, making everything go dark. A crack of thunder rang through the air and a spark of lightening illuminated the night sky. Suddenly, the Dragon King appeared next to Taotie, who immediately grabbed the rabbit again.

"I – I was just about to bring the rabbit to you, my lord ..." Taotie stammered.

"Take him to the place I told you to. I want to say a few words to my nemesis," the Dragon King said, looking Jack straight in the eye.

Not him again, thought Jack. Every time he saw the Dragon King, Jack felt his fists clench. The fact that he'd killed Jack's dad, Ju-Long, caused a rage to build inside of him. Jack longed to get rid of him for once and for all, but the Dragon King was like a bad smell that kept coming back.

"Ah, Tiger Warrior, here again." The Dragon King smiled and tapped his long-nailed fingers together. "I see that Taotie has done my bidding! What a delight it is to see its body complete once again. You know, I said it could eat whatever and whoever it pleases once it had captured the Jade Rabbit for me."

Princess Li stood next to Jack, her hands up ready to fight.

"So Taotie isn't going to eat the Jade Rabbit?" she said.

"Well, Taotie might eat the rabbit when we're done with him," said the Dragon King. "But first I need the rabbit to make the elixir of life for me. Then I will be immortal, and I shall command an army of immortals, and there will be no stopping me!" The Dragon King held a black jewel high in the air and in a flash of smoke, he was gone.

The sky crackled with lightning and it began to pour with rain. The stall owners wheeled their stalls away, the paper lanterns became soggy messes and the fire dragon was left abandoned on the floor. As Taotie scampered away clutching the Jade Rabbit, water began pooling on the ground. Jack quickly summoned Rat from the coin. He needed her power to control the weather.

"Rat, I need your help to stop this torrential rain," he said. "It's going to be hard to chase Taotie on Horse if the streets are all muddy."

Rat clapped her little pink paws

together and
concentrated.
Her power
was not often
called for, so
she was eager
to show Jack what
she could do. The rain
stopped, but then a tornado began to
whirl in circles.

"Oh no, Rat, that's not what I was
thinking!" Jack said.

By the time Rat had got the tornado to
subside, Taotie and the Jade Rabbit had
disappeared.

"Where do you think the Dragon King

told Taotie to take the Jade Rabbit?" Jack asked Li.

"I don't know, but it must be to do with making the elixir of life," Li replied. "And we can't let that happen!"

'You're telling me! Don't worry, we are going to stop this," Jack said. The thought of the Dragon King being able to live forever was unbearable. Jack had to find Taotie and save the Jade Rabbit – but how?

CHAPTER FIVE

Jack took the coin from his pocket and summoned the rest of the zodiac animals.

"We need your help to save the Jade Rabbit and stop the Dragon King," he told them.

"Use me!" said Tiger. "I have been looking forward to using my fireballs on the Dragon King – I've even been having dreams about it."

"I can make you invisible and we can use sssssstealth to get the rabbit back," Snake said.

Rooster flew up, wings flapping. "Use me! Use me! We can fly over that beast, peck its head and pluck the rabbit out from its grip. Taotie won't know what's hit him."

"All of those ideas sound great, but we need to know where Taotie is first," said Jack. "Goat, can you tap into Taotie's mind and see where it might be right now?"

Goat closed her eyes and Jack closed his too, trying to tap into her telepathic ability. As Jack tuned into Taotie's mind,

he saw some green bushes and mud,
but then all he could see were images
of food. There was fried fish with spring
onions, a sheep in a field, a basket full
of turnips, hot bowls of steaming white
rice and then … Jack saw himself and
the zodiac animals in a huge cooking pot

being made into a soup! He shuddered and opened his eyes. So did Goat, who ran behind Dragon.

"Taotie wants to eat all of us!" she bleated.

"It probably doesn't want to eat me," said Dragon confidently.

"No, it wants to eat you too," said Jack. "Taotie was dreaming of you in a cooking pot with the rest of us. But don't worry, we'll work together and we'll stop it. No one is going to make us into soup." Jack saw Pig gulp.

"We must go and speak to my father," said Li. "He knows what the ingredients of the elixir are and that might give us a clue to where Taotie has taken the Jade Rabbit."

"Brilliant idea," Jack replied. "Come on, let's go!"

When they reached the Jade Palace, they found the Emperor waiting in the throne room.

Chang'e was pacing up and down. Her face was pale with concern. "Where's the Jade Rabbit?" she cried as soon as she saw them.

"We weren't able to save the rabbit yet," Jack replied. "The Dragon King appeared and helped Taotie get away."

"No!" Chang'e exclaimed.

"It's OK. I think we can find them,"

said Jack. He turned to the Emperor. "But we need your help."

"Of course! I'll do anything I can to help you on this mission," the Jade Emperor replied.

"Father, the Dragon King got Taotie to take the Jade Rabbit because he wants him to make the elixir of life," Li explained. "He's planning on making himself immortal, and he's going to make all of his terrible creatures immortal too!"

"Oh, this is terrible!" the Emperor gasped.

"It's true, and we really need your help," said Jack. "Do you know where we can find the ingredients needed for the

elixir? We can try to catch them there."
Jack looked at the Emperor hopefully. He
was hugely relieved to see the Emperor
nod.

"The ingredients for the elixir are
a white jade pear, a mushroom of
eternity and a gemstone from the tree
of immortality," the Emperor said. "And
they can all be found in the magical
garden on the mountain of Kunlun. You
need to climb the mountain until you
reach the ledge with the trees. When you
get there, follow the river and you will
find the garden. Hurry! You must stop
them!"

"We will, Father. And don't worry,

we've got the Tiger Warrior!" said
Princess Li.

The Emperor gave Jack a grateful smile.

"Please be careful," Chang'e implored.

Back outside the palace, Jack hopped
on to Horse and put the other animals
back inside the coin.

"To the mountain!" he cried.

Li transformed into the Fenghuang and
flew above. As soon as they reached the
base of the mountain, Jack summoned
Rooster from the coin.

"I need you to fly me up there,"
he said, pointing to a tree-lined ledge
halfway up.

Once they had reached the ledge, Li

changed back into her human form. Jack took the coin from his pocket.

"ZODIAC!" he called, and the other animals all appeared.

"I'm so tired from all that flying," Li said, sitting down on the riverbank and rubbing her arms. "We have to be alert. Taotie will eat us all if he gets the chance, and we need to get the Jade Rabbit away from him without that happening."

The group followed the river deeper into the mountain, past the trees with the luscious green leaves. Soon they came upon the beautiful garden that the Jade Emperor had talked about.

Jack crouched low as they got closer. He could hear something ahead. He pulled back some large green leaves and there was the terrible Taotie. Its claw-like talons were prodding a reluctant-looking Jade Rabbit. Jack's mouth dropped open when he saw what was in the rabbit's paws – it was a white jade pear.

"He's got the pear!" Jack whispered to Li.

"Pear? Did someone say pear?" said Pig, snuffling hungrily.

"You can't eat it, it's magical," said Dog.

"What shall we do?" asked Li.

"There must be a way we can distract

Taotie and save the rabbit," said Jack.
"Without getting chewed up!"

"I've got an idea," said Rabbit. "I can
use my earthquake hop and bring down
the mountain."

Jack shook his head. "I'm sorry, Rabbit.
I know you would like to save one of

your own kind. But that sounds way too risky. Rocks could fall and hit us on the head."

"What about using Rooster to fly in and get the Jade Rabbit from the claws of Taotie?" said Li.

Jack looked at Rooster. His head was dropping and his feathers were bedraggled. "I think Rooster is too tired from flying up the mountain. And he can only go short distances."

"I wish I had some mooncakes," Pig said. "They always make me think better."

"Me too!" Monkey exclaimed, waving his long arms in the air.

Jack's face lit up. "Monkey, maybe I could harness your power, and extend my arms and grab the rabbit. And then I could use your athletic ability to swing away before he catches up with me."

"Yes, yes, use me!" Monkey jumped up and down with excitement.

"Hmm, I'm not sure having long arms is going to be enough to defeat Taotie," Dragon said.

"Monkey's power isn't strong enough,' said Tiger.

"Yes, his power is only good for stealing food," chortled Dog, and the other animals laughed.

They reminded Jack of Marcus and

 the way he teased him for not being good enough at gaming.

"Don't listen to them, Monkey," he said. "I think your powers are great."

"Sounds like it might work," said Princess Li. "But Taotie isn't going to give up the rabbit without a fight."

"Maybe we could distract Taotie instead?" said Pig. "If only we had some of those delicious mooncakes that it loves to gobble. They are so tasty..."

"Pig, you are a genius. But the mooncakes are all the way down in the village," Jack said.

"I could fly to get them," said Li.

"But you're exhausted – we all are, from the climb," Jack replied. "There must be an easier way."

"What if we just send him pictures of the mooncakes instead?" said Goat. "I can use telepathy to make him crave the food and then hopefully he'll go and look for it and leave the garden."

"Great plan, Goat! Let's do it!" Jack said.

"Are you sure you don't need my

powers?" Monkey asked, looking dejected.

"Not this time, Monkey," Jack replied. "But I'm sure I'll need them soon."

Goat closed her eyes and started to send images of delicious mooncakes straight to Taotie's mind. Jack and the others watched as drool started trickling from the monster's mouth.

"Yes!" Jack whispered as the monster left the Jade Rabbit and started sniffing around the edges of the garden in search of mooncakes. It was working! Goat's mind control was really making Taotie hungry. It used its clawed hands to scour through the bushes.

"Taotie loves mooncakes even more than Monkey and I do,' Pig said as he watched the monster's desperate search.

On the other side of the garden, the Jade Rabbit plucked a mushroom from the soil. This was their chance!

"OK, on my count ... three ... two ... one ..." Jack whispered. "Let's get the rabbit!" He ran out of the bushes and lifted the Jade Rabbit off the ground. He was about to turn and head back to Li and the other Zodiac animals when a deafening clap of thunder rang out. Jack's heart sank. That sound meant one thing. The Dragon King was there!

"I'll turn into the Fenghuang," Princess

Li whispered to Jack.

"Going somewhere?" laughed the Dragon King. In his hand was the black jewel he'd been holding earlier. The Dragon King had many different jewels, all with different powers. Jack wondered which power he would be using against them today. The Dragon King pointed the jewel at the bushes where Princess Li was hiding. Before she could turn into the Fenghuang, she was dragged by an invisible power straight into the clutches of the Dragon King. He held on to her wrist with his bony fingers.

"Let me go!" Li cried.

"I don't think so," the Dragon King

replied. "Not while your friend has the
Jade Rabbit." He looked at Jack and gave
an evil cackle.

CHAPTER SIX

"Let her go!" shouted Jack. The Jade Rabbit trembled in his arms.

"Please don't give me back to the monster!" the Jade Rabbit pleaded.

"You'll pay for this!" Princess Li yelled, trying to escape the Dragon King's grasp, but he was too strong.

The black jewel must be giving him extra powers, Jack thought.

"Release me immediately," Li cried.

"I don't think you are in a position to make demands, Princess," the Dragon King said before turning to Jack. "So, Tiger Warrior, what are you going to do now? The Jade Emperor will be most unhappy if you give up his beloved princess."

Jack scowled at him.

"There's only one thing you can do," the Dragon King continued. "Give me the Jade Rabbit and I will hand back the Princess." His eyes glinted with evil.

Jack wasn't about to let Princess Li die, but he knew that if the Dragon King had an elixir of immortality, then everyone in the Jade Kingdom would be doomed. Not only would the Dragon King live forever, but he could also create an army of immortal monsters. The Tiger Warrior had powers, but trying to stop immortals would be very difficult indeed. Jack knew he had to do something, and fast. Too much was at stake. If the monsters took over the Jade Kingdom, it wouldn't be long before they conquered Jack's world too!

Taotie was still rummaging around searching for more mooncakes, which was a good thing for Jack because it was one less monster to face. Taking on the Dragon King and Taotie at the same time would be a huge challenge.

"Well? Are you going to give me the rabbit?" the Dragon King asked. "I shall give you to the count of three. ONE ... TWO ..."

"Don't do it, Jack!" shouted Princess Li. "I'd rather perish than let him make an elixir that gives him immortality. It's too big of a risk. My father will think of something."

"Your father is pathetic! I'd like to see him stop me," the Dragon King boomed.

Jack bent down and touched Goat's head. He needed to send a telepathic message to Li: *Trust me, and go along with my plan. I'm going to let the Jade*

Rabbit go, and when I say now, I need you to distract the Dragon King. Jack

winked at Li and she nodded that she had understood. Thankfully, the Dragon King didn't suspect a thing.

"Fine. I'm going to let the Jade Rabbit go," Jack said, "but you must keep your side of the bargain and release Princess Li."

"Excellent, excellent. You have a deal,"

the Dragon King replied, but he laughed a laugh so sinister that Jack felt the hairs on his arm prickle. "Taotie, stop messing about and get the rabbit from the boy for me," the Dragon King ordered.

Taotie scampered over and Jack released the Jade Rabbit into the claws of the beast.

"Now find the rest of the ingredients," the monster growled, poking the rabbit.

The Jade Rabbit placed the mushroom and the white jade pear into a large stone bowl, then hopped over to the other side of the garden.

"So, when are you going to keep your side of the deal and release the Princess?" Jack asked. He knew full well that the Dragon King could not be trusted, so he sent a quick message to Goat: *The next part of my plan is about to take place and Monkey needs to be ready.*

Goat sent Jack a telepathic message back: *I'll get him ready, Jack. You just give the word.*

Jack nodded, but inside he felt sick with nerves. He really hoped his plan would work. If the Dragon King won this battle, they'd never be able to defeat him!

CHAPTER SEVEN

Jack watched as the Jade Rabbit hopped over to a beautiful tree on the other side of the garden. Green-blue gemstones hung from its branches and they glistened in the moonlight like jewels in a computer game.

"The tree of immortality!" Li gasped.

The Dragon King held on to her tighter. "That's right, my dear, and soon I shall be the Dragon King of immortality! It has a wonderful ring to it, doesn't it?"

"Now!" Jack shouted.

Li nodded and she stomped on the Dragon King's feet with all her might. The Dragon King howled with pain as he hopped from foot to foot, trying to soothe himself.

Jack knew this was his chance. He needed the longest reach possible if he was to save the Jade Rabbit and get the mysterious black jewel from the Dragon King.

Jack tossed the Jade Coin into the air and shouted "MONKEY TRANSFORM!" In an instant Monkey was at his side. Jack thought of all the times Marcus had teased him for losing at *Jungle Quest* and he felt his arms begin to tingle as he harnessed Monkey's power. He had become one with the creature that was teased by the other animals for not having an amazing power.

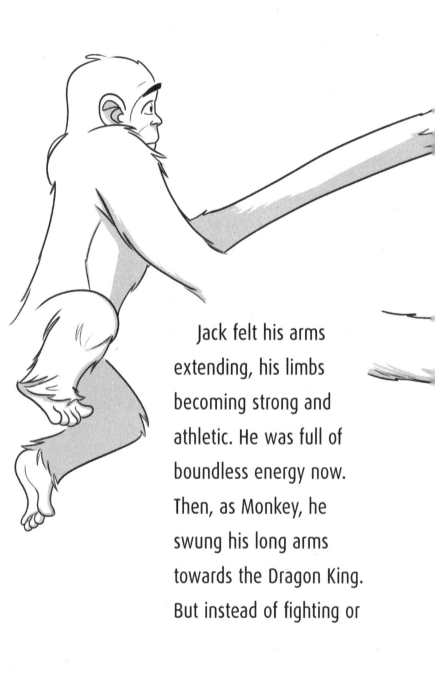

Jack felt his arms
extending, his limbs
becoming strong and
athletic. He was full of
boundless energy now.
Then, as Monkey, he
swung his long arms
towards the Dragon King.
But instead of fighting or

trying to get the jewel, Jack had another plan. He began tickling the Dragon King, who was not expecting such an attack. Jack knew that Monkey's cheeky nature was just what was needed in this situation. The Dragon King was expecting a fight, but what he wasn't expecting was to be tickled. The Dragon King tried to stop himself laughing, his sharp teeth glistening in the light of the full moon as he opened his mouth.

"No! I shall not be tickled. I am the Dragon King! I shall – oh no, not there!"

Jack used his long monkey arms to grab the Dragon King and lay him on his back, then he held up the Dragon's King's feet and began to tickle them.

"No, not my feet!" the Dragon King cried, before shrieking with laughter.

Jack wound his super-extendable arms around the Dragon King, causing him to loosen his grip on Li.

As soon as she was free from his grasp, Li transformed into the Fenghuang and soared into the air. Jack saw that Taotie had turned his attention back to the poor Jade Rabbit, who had a gemstone from the tree of immortality in his paw. If that ended up in the bowl, then it was all over. The Dragon King would have his elixir of immortality. Jack used one of his very long arms to grab the white jade pear from the bowl. He lobbed it into the air just like a basketball in *Jungle Quest* and shouted, "Taotie! Dinner!"

Taotie turned towards Jack. Its large eyes blinked once and then twice. When it saw the white jade pear, the monster

opened its mouth and gobbled it down just like that.

"Yes, a three pointer!" Jack yelled, imagining he'd just won the basketball game.

"No!" the Dragon King wailed.

"Game over!" Jack laughed.

"Jack! Watch out!" Fenghuang shouted from up in the sky.

Jack turned and saw the Dragon King marching towards him. He was clearly in a rage!

"How dare you upset my plans?" he bellowed.

But then Taotie began to splutter and heave. The white jade pear was clearly making him feel sick.

"You stupid beast! How could you eat one of the ingredients?" the Dragon King yelled, and Taotie cowered. "I will take away your body again, you useless creature!" The Dragon King held up the black jewel and pointed it at Taotie. In a flash of lightning, his body vanished and his eyeless head dropped to the floor.

Before the Dragon King could do anything else, the Fenghuang swooped down and snatched the black jewel from his hand. She threw it in Jack's direction. The Dragon King sprang forward and tried to grab the jewel before Jack could catch it. But Jack's amazing long arms zoomed forward, grabbed the black jewel and smashed it hard into the Jade Rabbit's stone bowl. The jewel shattered into smithereens. The Dragon King looked at his hands.

"No! My power is fading!" he cried. He glared at Jack, who had now transformed back into his human self. "You might have won this battle, but I will be back!"

There was a loud clap of thunder and the Dragon King was gone.

Taotie's head groaned and slunk off into the bushes.

"At least it won't be able to eat anything or anyone again," Li said as she changed back into her human form and raised her hand for a high-five.

As they high-fived, Jack gave a sigh of

relief. He hated to think of what might have happened if the Dragon King had succeeded in his evil plan. Who knows what mayhem Taotie would have caused if it had become immortal and crossed over into Jack's world. Especially in the Chinese supermarket, with its rows and rows of delicious mooncakes of all kinds. Unlike Marcus, Taotie was not a fussy eater at all!

"We did it!" Jack cried, and the zodiac animals all cheered.

"And you used my powers!" Monkey called as he swung through the trees in celebration.

"Yes, Monkey," Jack said. "Without

your long arms and athletic abilities, I wouldn't have been able to defeat the Dragon King and get Taotie to swallow the white jade pear. You might not have fire power or invisibility, but Chang'e will be so grateful to you."

The zodiac animals all nodded in agreement and Monkey beamed with pride.

Li scooped the Jade Rabbit into her arms. "Come on, let's get the rabbit back to the palace, and then we need to have some mooncakes.

We deserve them after what we've been through!"

"Yes, we certainly do!" Monkey exclaimed.

CHAPTER EIGHT

Li transformed into the Fenghuang so
she could carry the Jade Rabbit back to
the palace. Jack rode on Horse as fast as
he could. He wanted to be there when
the Jade Rabbit was returned. When they
arrived, Jack summoned the other zodiac
animals out of the coin. They were happy
to see the splendour of the Jade Palace
again. A crowd had gathered outside,

anxiously waiting for news.

"Cock-a-doodle-doo! We're back!" Rooster announced loudly. "The Tiger Warrior saved the Jade Rabbit!"

The crowd cheered.

"With the help of Monkey's power!" added Jack. He gave Monkey a high-five and rubbed his palm after, because he had forgotten just how strong Monkey's hands were.

Monkey grinned. "I guess I am a useful animal after all, and these long arms of mine can be a superpower too."

Jack laughed. "Of course they can. And you've taught me some new moves – like the super slam dunk!"

Everyone laughed and Monkey swung happily from pillar to pillar outside the Jade Palace.

Chang'e and the Jade Emperor rushed out of the main entrance, both smiling in relief. The Jade Rabbit hopped down from the Fenghuang's talons and into the arms of his beloved moon goddess.

"Oh, I'm so glad you're here! I thought I'd lost you forever to that foul beast," Chang'e cried. "I couldn't bear the thought of going back to the moon without you. It would have been too lonely." The moon goddess hugged the rabbit tightly.

"The Tiger Warrior and the Princess showed the Dragon King and his ugly beast who was boss!" Pig said proudly.

"What happened to Taotie?" asked the Jade Emperor.

"The Dragon King took away his body again," Jack replied.

"So his head is floating about on Kunlun," Li said, transforming back into her human self.

"Ah, I see," said the Jade Emperor. "Let's hope that means more peaceful times. Well done, you two and, of course, the zodiac animals." The Jade Emperor smiled at the animals. "Now let the celebrations continue. The moon goddess and her rabbit friend are only here for one night after all!"

Everyone cheered and the lanterns were lit once more. The Moon Festival carried on into the early hours of the morning. The zodiac animals and Li feasted on mooncakes and other delicious food. But Jack only had a small slice of one of the cakes.

"How come you're not eating more?" Princess Li asked.

"I need to save space for when I get home." Jack grinned. "Yeye has bought so many different types of mooncake for us to try, I don't want to be full up!"

"I'll eat the rest of Jack's mooncake," said Pig, snuffling over. Jack happily gave him the rest of his egg-yolk filled cake.

"And talking of Yeye, I think it's time I went home," said Jack. He had had quite the adventure and now he looked forward to spending some time with his family in the garden. Plus he had some new moves to show off in *Jungle Quest* and he couldn't wait to take on Marcus.

"Thank you once again, Tiger Warrior, for protecting our realm," said the Jade Emperor. "Send warm wishes to your grandfather."

"I will," Jack replied.

"Yes, and thank you for bringing me back my best friend," said Chang'e.

The Jade Rabbit hopped over to Jack and nuzzled against his leg in thanks.

"See you again soon," Princess Li said to Jack. "Take care of yourself."

"I will, see you." And with his final goodbye, Jack tossed the Jade Coin into the air.

It span around and around, and golden light cascaded around it.

"HOME!" Jack shouted. A portal opened and Jack stepped through.

Jack found himself back in his bedroom. He looked at his bedside clock. The time hadn't moved at all. He was still supposed to be upstairs getting another controller so he could play *Jungle Quest* with Marcus. But little did his boastful cousin know that being Monkey and learning how to do the super slam dunk had given Jack an advantage. Jack went downstairs and saw that everyone apart from Yeye was in the garden. His mum had laid the table with watermelon, pomelo slices and other yummy food. Jack was glad he hadn't filled up in the Jade Kingdom.

He found Yeye in the kitchen.

"You'll never guess who I met tonight," Jack said.

"Was it someone of great beauty and her little white furry friend?" Yeye said with glee.

"How did you know?" Jack gasped.

"You look like you've just got back from an adventure." Yeye chuckled. "I know that glint in your eye – your father used to have it whenever he got back from a mission. Are you all right?"

"Yeah, it was a close call though. The Dragon King got Taotie to kidnap the Jade Rabbit! He wanted him to make the elixir of immortality. But we managed to get him back," Jack said.

"Oh my!" Yeye exclaimed. "If the Dragon King had got that elixir of immortality, then all would have been lost. Jack, you have just saved the world. Well done!" Yeye gave him a hug.

"Thanks, Yeye. But now I'm starving!"

Jack's mouth was watering just like Taotie's, but thankfully with less drool dangling from his mouth.

"We're going to eat in about ten minutes," said Yeye. "We're just waiting for the duck to finish roasting."

"Jack! Where are you?" Marcus called from the living room. "I'm waiting to beat you at *Jungle Quest*."

"Go on, go and have some fun with

your cousin," Yeye said, patting Jack on the back.

Normally, Jack wouldn't have described gaming with Marcus as fun, but now he couldn't wait to try out his new super slam dunk move. He hurried through to the living room and sat beside Marcus on the sofa.

"It's time for the Basketball Arena battleground," Marcus announced. "As it's the Moon Festival, I might let you score one basket. I'll even let you choose your avatar."

"You're on!" said Jack, choosing the monkey avatar. After harnessing Monkey's powers, he felt that he understood how to use it much better.

'You've chosen the monkey avatar? You know that is the absolute worst one?" Marcus teased. "You are going to get beaten so badly, worse than you've ever been beaten before!"

Jack laughed. Little did Marcus know that he'd just faced real enemies. Enemies that would literally eat you alive! As the cousins started doing battle, Jack wasn't worried about losing any more and that made him play much better. As he used the controller to dodge the flying pineapples, he had an idea. Instead of dodging the pineapples, what if he caught one and dunked it into the palm tree to try and score some points? He'd never even tried it before. When Marcus's avatar, the King of the Jungle, threw a pineapple at Jack's avatar, he used the controls with ease. He caught the pineapple and jumped up high, dunking it into the tallest palm tree. "100 points" flashed on to the screen.

"How did you do that?" Marcus said.

"Just luck, I guess," Jack replied with a grin.

Again and again, Marcus lobbed pineapples at Jack's avatar, and again and again, Jack used his new super slam dunk move. After just a few minutes, it was game over and Jack had won.

Marcus slung his controller down on the sofa. "That was a great move," he muttered. "You'll have to show me how to do it."

Jack's grin grew. He never thought he'd see the day his cousin would ask him for help. He rubbed the Jade Coin in his pocket and silently thanked Monkey.

"Food is ready!" Yeye called, coming into the room with a plate of roast duck.

Jack and Marcus followed him outside. The garden looked beautiful with lanterns hanging all around the edges. The food looked and smelled amazing.

"Tuck in!" said Laura.

Jack handed Marcus one of the

ice cream mooncakes and he took a
traditional one with lotus paste.

"Those were your father's favourite,"

Yeye said, putting his arm around Jack.

As Jack bit into the cake, he looked up at the moon. For a second, he thought he saw a flash of light. He squinted, and there in the centre of the moon he saw the Jade Rabbit and the moon goddess, beaming down. Jack grinned. They were watching over him after all.

THE END

*Read on for a sneak peek of
Jack's next adventure*

PROLOGUE

It was the dead of night and the only sound that could be heard was the croaking of crickets in the Jade Palace gardens. Despite the palace looking peaceful and still, something - or someone - was darting around in the shadows, not wanting to be seen. A masked figure, wearing a cloak as black as the night sky, tiptoed silently along corridors and through doorways until they reached the large, engraved wooden door of the Jade Emperor's private chamber. No one was allowed in that area apart from those very close to the Jade Emperor, and it was protected by the Emperor's special guards. But the stranger had worked out that the guards drank calming oolong tea before their shift, so administering the sleeping potion was easy.

The stranger turned the corner, then stopped. They stood as still as a statue until they heard bodies thudding to the floor, one after the other. The potion had worked. *The special guards aren't that special,* the intruder thought to themselves. The subdued guards lay across the floor outside the Emperor's sleeping quarters – one on either side of the door. Both women snored loudly, their hair hanging limply over their closed eyes. Their weapons remained sheathed.

"Sleep well. Now it's time for the fun part," whispered the hooded figure, amused by the scene. This was too easy. The intruder crept towards the Emperor's door, slowly pushing it open a little at a time. Then they edged towards the Emperor's bed, over to the spectacular golden lamp that flickered away in the corner. The figure reached into their cloak and pulled out an orange gemstone the size of their hand. "I have reached the Lamp of Protection, Master," the figure whispered into the jewel. The Dragon King's face appeared in the gemstone's shiny flat surface. His eyes were wide with malice and satisfaction.

"Excellent," he said. "Now you must extinguish the flame." The intruder did as they were told, puckering their lips together and giving an almighty blow. Darkness moved into every corner of the room as the light went out. A cold breeze swept through the chamber, bringing with it a chill. The Jade Emperor turned over in his sleep and pulled the silk bedsheets up to his chin.

"Now the lamp is out, his god-like powers will drain away until he is as vulnerable as a newborn baby. I can finally return and rule as I was always meant to. Let chaos reign! Vengeance will finally be mine!" The Dragon King's eyes gleamed from within the jewel as it caught the moonlight. "Now go – hurry out of the palace and prepare for the next stage. Let's see the ultimate justice carried out!" With a cackle, the Dragon's King's face was gone. And so too was the intruder. In the palace, the Jade Emperor and the guards slept on, unaware that they were all in terrible danger . . .

ANIMAL CHARACTERISTICS

RAT

Rats might have a bit of a bad reputation in books and films, but they're number one when it comes to the zodiac. People born in the Year of the Rat are quick-witted, persuasive and very smart. They have excellent taste but can be known to be a little greedy!

OX

The Ox is patient and powerful. People born in this year are known for being kind to others. While they can be a little stubborn, people born in the Year of Ox make the best friends – they can always be counted on to protect the ones that they love.

TIGER

Tigers are famously strong and majestic, so it's no wonder that Tiger Warriors like Jack and his yeye are born in this year. People born in the Year of the Tiger are courageous but are known to be a bit moody too!

RABBIT

Forget the cute bunnies, people born in the Year of the Rabbit are the cool kids! Known for being popular and sincere and for always helping others, rabbits feel most at home with lots of guests around.

DRAGON

If you're born in this year, you're very lucky indeed! The charismatic dragon is revered all over China. Those born in the Year of the Dragon are energetic and fearless, but can be a bit selfish ... No wonder the Dragon King thinks he should be the leader of the Jade Kingdom!

SNAKE

Those born in the Year of the Sssnake are quiet, charming and smart. They're very good with money, but be careful, they're known for getting quite jealous!

People born in the Year of the Horse are very energetic and love to travel. But remember, they do not like waiting. They want to bolt right out of the gates!

Also known as the Year of the Sheep, people born in this year can be a little shy but are great at understanding people. They're happy to be left alone with their thoughts, and maybe think a bit too much about what others think of them.

MONKEY

Monkeys are a lot of fun to be around. Active and entertaining, people born in this year are great at making people laugh! They like to listen to others but can sometimes lack self-control.

ROOSTER

Hard-working and practical, those born in the Year of the Rooster have a bit of a reputation for being perfectionists. They're very reliable – you can always trust a rooster.

DOG

People born in the Year of the Dog are amazing friends and great at sharing. They sometimes get a little moody, but they're famous for being good, honest people.

PIG

What a great sign to be in! People born in the Year of the Pig are known for being luxurious! They love learning and helping others.

Q&A with Maisie Chan

Taotie loves to eat – what is your favourite food?
I love dim sum! Dim sum is often steamed or fried food. It might be fish or meat dumplings. Or long rice rolls filled with pork or prawns. Or seafood fried into small parcels. I love the variety of foods that can be served in the bamboo towers. And I really like that it's a sociable meal where you talk and share food together. I have had dim sum alone and it's not the same.

If you could only have one kind of mooncake, which would it be?
I really like puddings and cakes with custard in them! So for me, it would have to be a mooncake filled with custard that pours out like lava!

Which animal would you want to live on the moon with?
I think it would have to be a dog. They're loyal and fun. You could play fetch with them if you throw moon rocks. And if it gets a bit chilly at night you can cuddle up in their fur and keep warm.

About Maisie Chan

 Maisie Chan is a children's author from Birmingham. When she was growing up, Maisie had no books that featured Chinese role models, so she became a children's author to change that. She even studied why there were not many Chinese role models in film at universities in Birmingham and America.

Maisie has been a storyteller in the past and entertained children in libraries, museums and schools with her favourite Chinese myths and legends. She currently lives in Glasgow and enjoys practising yoga, walks around the parks and visiting the seaside.

MOON FESTIVAL FACT FILE

The Moon Festival, also known as the Mid-Autumn Festival, takes place on the fifteenth day of the eighth lunar month and is always celebrated on a full moon.

Chinese emperors used to worship the moon; they believed it would bring a plentiful harvest the following year. Later, this custom spread to regular citizens who began to appreciate the moon when it was at its brightest.

It is the second most popular festival after the Lunar New Year celebrations and is celebrated in many countries in East and Southeast Asia.

The full moon symbolises reunion and that is why families get together, worship the moon and eat mooncakes. They are gifted to friends and relatives a few weeks before the actual day. Today, you can get all kinds of mooncakes. Most are round but occasionally you might find a square one! They can be sweet or savoury and some traditional fillings include: lotus seed paste, red bean paste and salted egg yolks. However, nowadays you can get ice cream ones and even jelly ones!

One of the most famous stories linked to the moon festival is about the moon goddess Chang'e and her husband, Hou Yi, an excellent archer. He had been given the elixir of immortality but he wanted to be human so he could stay with his wife. But a rival archer tried to take the elixir from his house. Chang'e drank it and then became immortal instead. Her new home became the moon and the Jade Rabbit became her companion. Her husband offered her favourite cakes up to the moon to show her how much he missed her.

HOW TO MAKE A PAPER LANTERN

YOU'LL NEED:

Paper

Scissors

Tape

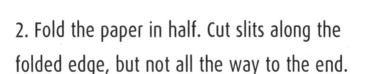

1. Cut off a strip of the end of your paper. This will be your handle.

2. Fold the paper in half. Cut slits along the folded edge, but not all the way to the end.

3. Take the two ends of the paper and wrap them around to make a tube. Tape the two ends together.

4. Tape the handle to the top and enjoy!

CIRCLE WORD SEARCH

Help Jack find all the hidden Zodiac animals in this word search!

☐Rat ☐Ox ☐Tiger ☐Rabbit ☐Dragon ☐Snake
☐Horse ☐Goat ☐Monkey ☐Rooster ☐Dog ☐Pig

HOW-TO-DRAW GRID

How to draw Jack and Li! Copy their pictures on to the grid. Some of it has already been done for you.

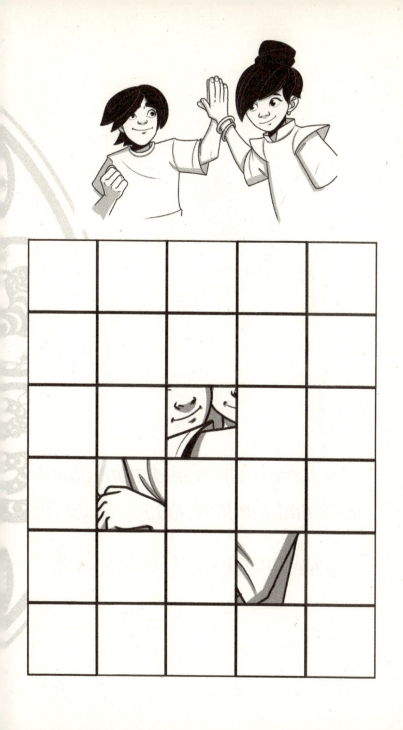

For fun activities and more about Jack and the Jade Kingdom, go to:

www.orchardseriesbooks.co.uk